T5-AXC-513

THE SHOES OF MAIDANEK

John Roth	Clairmont McKenna College Clairmont, California
Richard L. Rubenstein	Florida State University Tallahassee, Florida
Ann Weiss	Rosemont, Pennsylvania

THE SHOES OF MAIDANEK

Arnold P. Goldstein

Illustrated by
Mark Sherman

Studies in the Shoah

Volume III

University Press of America®, Inc.
4720 Boston Way
Lanham, Maryland 20706

3 Henrietta Street
London WC2E 8LU England

Printed in the United States of America
British Cataloging in Publication Information Available

Library of Congress Cataloging-in-Publication Data

Goldstein, Arnold P.
The shoes of Maidanek / Arnold P. Goldstein ;
illustrated by Mark Sherman.
p. cm. — (Studies in the Shoah)
1. Holocaust, Jewish (1939–1945)—Fiction.
2. Maidanek (Poland : Concentration camp)—Fiction.
I. Title. II. Series.
PS3557.0387S53 1992 813'.54—dc20 92–7409 CIP

ISBN 0–8191–8663–5 (cloth : alk. paper)
ISBN 0–8191–8664–3 (pbk. : alk. paper)

The paper used in this publication meets the minimum requirements of American National Standard for Information Sciences—Permanence of Paper for Printed Library Materials, ANSI Z39.48–1984.

...from the earliest days, from the fourth century, the sixth century, the missionaries of Christianity had said in effect to the Jews: "You may not live among us as Jews." The secular rulers who followed them from the middle ages then decided: "You may not live among us," and the Nazis finally decreed: "You may not live."

Raul Hilberg

The Destruction of the European Jews

To the life that was, and to the lives that could have been.

A.P.G.

Acknowledgement

Survivor testimonies bearing witness to the events of life and death in the Holocaust were the raw materials from which both the spirit and substance of this book were drawn. Though given voice in a diary and a character created by me, almost all of the events depicted herein actually occurred in one or another of the Nazi death camps. Those relatively few created de novo fully reflect both the sense and intent of these testimonies. My deepest appreciation, therefore, is offered to the survivors for the accounts they have courageously provided. My hope is that this extension of their Holocaust-burdened pasts, as portrayed in the present book through the eyes of one adolescent prisoner, will serve to carry forward their hopes for a Holocaust-free future.

As the death camp diary which follows unfolds, I ask the reader to step through its barbed wire fencing, and enter the nether world of Maidanek. Should you wonder how such a diary could actually have been written, given the severe privations and repressions of camp life, I ask that you suspend such literal wonderment. It was not written on paper from the cement bags used to build the crematoria. It was not written on pilfered scraps of message paper, or old written orders, or labels of cans from the camp kitchen. I offer instead a more spiritual origin, for this diary was written on the tablets of eternity, its ink the blood of the six million. So, too, its drawings, the sketches of a young man never to be an old man, seeking to capture the uncapturable.

Where was it stored? How did it survive for fifty years? In a crack in the ceiling beams over its keeper's head? In the ticking of his spartan straw mattress? No. The diary lived for half a century, as it will live for another half, in the depths of determination, the haunts of hope, the hearts of survivors, and the shoes of Maidanek.

Foreword

The systematic extermination of European Jewry ceased nearly a half century ago. The Shoah's effects, however, continue to be keenly felt. Scholars seek its lessons, artists attempt to portray its nameless horror. Philosophers search for meaning and theologians speak of God's relationship to the catastrophe. Sifting the wreckage, Jews seek a clue to their identity and the meaning of their destiny. Yet, how can a nonwitness speak of the event? If there is one rule concerning writings about the Holocaust, it has to do with humility. Confronting the enormity of the death camps and the unspeakable agony of those who suffered there, requires a two-fold admission; that what happened must be written about and that it can never be adequately conveyed.

The Shoah has, however, entered the public domain. Anyone is free to say whatever they wish. Frequently this is done with little or no reference to historical data. No requirement exists that those who study and write about the Shoah must visit the sites of former death camps. This is indeed a pity. Auschwitz, Buchenwald, Maidanek, Treblinka, these are the names of some of the infamous landmarks on National Socialism's map of Hell. Perhaps experiencing their eerie silence would have a transformative effect. Listening to this silence is far more difficult, and important, than trying to describe it. The death camps hold a mirror to the face of culture.

Arnold P. Goldstein, is one who had made a pilgrimage to Maidanek. He went both for personal and professional reasons. Expressing his Jewishness, the author's trip revealed as well his concern about the unending persistence of antisemitism in particular and aggression in general. This led him to attempt to imagine the unimaginable anguish of a Jew enmeshed in the Nazi web of death. Writing this young man's story, Professor Goldstein underscores the murderous particularity of the Jewish experience. Abandoned and alone, the youth embraces his identity even while on the edge of an abyss.

I believe that The Shoes of Maidanek is the harbinger of a new genre. This genre must come into being if the Holocaust is to be rescued from triviality and distortion. The ranks of the survivors are growing thinner. Deniers and falsifiers are growing stronger. Popular culture continues to distort. Holocaust education and literature are necessary to sensitize people to an event they have not experienced, but whose effects could destroy them. In our time, there is no more urgent task then combatting antisemitism and other forms of hatred. It is in this way that we can possibly reclaim a vestige of human dignity.

Alan L. Berger, Director
Jewish Studies Program
Syracuse University

October 16

Is there shit up my nose? Did someone shove shit up my nose? I can't get the smell to stop, even breathing through my mouth. I thought people get used to bad smells, but this gets worse and worse each hour. There must be 150 people in this train car, and it smells like they all shit. Our living room at home has about as much space, and it seemed crowded when twenty people came to Hilda's party. It's so crowded here that when someone pees in his pants, the pee rolls down the legs of three different people.

We're going I don't know where, to maybe even more terrible things than the daymares that happened at home, but all I can think of is shit, pee, drink and eat. We haven't had a drink since...I don't remember. My tongue feels like the leather of my shoe. What are people peeing if they don't have water for two days? I watched a man try to drink his own urine. Is that next for me? This morning the train stopped, and a man in our car from Sanniki Street was ordered to take the shit pail to a stream 50 meters from the train and bring back drinking water. But he tried to run away and they shot him, and left him and the pail in the stream.

When I think beyond my tongue, my nose, my stomach, I am really scared!!! And very, very sad. When they came to round up our block, grandpa couldn't hear too well, or move too fast, and a butcher bastard killed him. A shout, a loud bang, and an instant small red circle on grandpa's forehead, and grandpa, who would live forever, was dead. I never saw a dead person before. I was a death virgin. And now there's grandpa, and Mr. Stern beaten to death at the corner, the baby hidden in the knapsack who cried out at the Umshlagplatz. God, oh God, they stuck the bayonet into the sack over and over till it was a bloody rag. And then they beat the father carrying it to death. And the three bodies just dumped off the train when it stopped this morning. I'm a death virgin no more.

Everyone has a horror story - arrest, beating, marching, clothes off, fingers or sticks stuck up asses and cunts searching for hidden jewelry or coins, hope for resettlement, fear for painful death, despair for loved ones. The lady next to poppa says she was just walking down the Street with her little son, and he ran ahead around the corner. When she caught up he had been grabbed by a Ukrainian police. She explained, protested, demanded her child, but the police said "How can we be sure he is your child?" And they put both of them on the train. The boy is so thirsty he licks his mama's sweat, and the side wall of the train!

But mostly the cows in this cattle car don't talk. They stay quiet, or they pray, or moan, or weep, or curse, or tear their hair, or make "death bed" confessions. One man on the other side of the car cried out about stealing money, and fucking women, and being sorry, and not wanting to die. We, the cows, have crossed to the other side. We have the aloneness of the dead. The Polish railroad workers I see through the slats laugh, and smoke, and point. The car like ours at the train siding had scrawled in chalk on it "Danger! Consignment of dirty Jews. Hands off!"

Sometime this morning (I think it was morning) the train stopped and they shoved another dozen fellow Jews into our car. Do we look like them? They still move, but are ghosts. Do we look like them!! They tell of the Germans shooting randomly into their group, of one emptying a baby's bottle to see if something was hidden in the milk, of street hunting, house raiding, beatings, and on and on. I think I may go mad myself. The train whistle sounds, and I hear it in my bones. It is the saddest sound I've ever heard.

We are now in our third day, and everything is worse, worse, worse. A lady near Hilda was nursing her baby and had no more milk. She cried, and cried, and hardly any tears came. Then she pressed the baby to her breast and kept it there. And soon the baby had died from not breathing. We are all going insane in here. I am most worried about Hilda. Whatever I say to her, she answers "I never did anybody harm." Is she crazy already? My poor Hilda.

My mother and father stay close, and talk only in whispers. I hear them talk about a terrible thing. They have cyanide pills. Where did you they get them?

How did they hide them? And, oh God, what do they plan. Is that to be our end?

October 17

I once had a long talk with Boris, my Catholic friend, about what happens after people die and he told me all about hell. It sounded horrible - violence, meanness, fires, death and no escape. Dear friend Boris, you were right...and it is here. The train stopped suddenly early this morning, the doors were opened, and a day in hell began.

Diary, I don't know if I can put it all down straight, because it is a jumble, and happened so fast, and my mind gets blank at times. The doors were opened and there was great noise and confusion. SS and other police with whips, guns, and vicious dogs yelled at us and pulled us from the train. One woman dropped her purse, and when she stopped and bent down to get it, a guard smashed her over the head and yelled she was holding things up. A man ducked under the train car and started running away, and they shot him. It was terrible. There was an awful smell in the air, not shit but a kind of putrid burning smell. What could it be? A couple kept holding onto each other, very, very tight, and the guards had trouble pulling them apart. He hit the man and the lady bit him. Two other SS ran over, held them down one on top of the other, and put a revolver to the man's head and shot both of them with one bullet. I was terrified. I even shit in my pants.

Momma tried to keep us all together, but we got separated when they made all the woman and children and old people go to one line, and all the men and older boys to another. I did stay with poppa, but Hilda and momma went off. The last I saw momma was waving to poppa with one arm, and pointing hard to her left shoulder. And Hilda, like some poor sick lamb, shuffled away, head down.

They took all our stuff and I mean all. Not just the brown suitcase and the big package poppa had tied together, but our jewelry (even my precious Bar Mitzvah ring) and our clothes. They made us get naked, looked up our asses, shaved off our hair, sprayed us with awful smelling stuff, and then threw us zebra clothing to put on. Has all this happened? Am I in a dream? Did I really see a man tell a guard to go fuck himself, and the guard stick his gun in the man's mouth and pull the trigger? Was that really a body hanging on the barbed wire fence? Did the fat SS man really piss on the old man he had knocked on the ground, and then choke him with his own tie? I sat with poppa when our hair was being cut. The man doing it knew poppa from the tailor shop, and said terrible, terrible things to us. He said this place, Maidanek, is a factory, a factory for death. Those who can't work are killed. If you look healthy enough, the barber said, they work you, but they work you to death. I can't bear the pain. Momma! Hilda! All the women and children he said are killed, right away. Can it be? Killed? Momma! Hilda! Poppa just sat there, looking older than grandpa. Boris, the hell you described was heaven compared to this.

October 18

Last year at this time the rules I had to live by were raise my hand in class, keep in line at the movie, ask permission to leave the table at home, and treat girls with respect. If I didn't, I'd get scolded. Now my rules are have no money or jewelry, have no food from outside this hell, don't damage prisoner goods stolen by the Reich. If I do, I'll get shot. And more. If I don't make my straw bed flat and smooth, keep the river of mud off my shoes, keep the buttons on my shirt, take my hat off to all SS, always pretend to understand them and never ask a question, I will be whipped. Also, stay at least two yards from the barbed-wire fence; sleep only in my shirt - no pants, cap or underwear; shit in this box not that one; don't keep my collar raised; and so many more I can't remember.

My friends then were Boris, Stefan, Pawel, Erich, and Albin. And they were friends - for play, for talks, for doing something and for doing nothing. Here there is poppa and no one else. We are zugangi, the new arrivals, and this makes us shit even to many other prisoners. How could they not care; how could they become so hard?

Then I slept in a warm bed, lived in a sunny room, ate momma's great cooking, played in our own small yard. Here I sleep on a hard bunk of boards, having night long nightmares, interrupted by strangers screaming, moaning, coughing, farting, cursing, fighting. I'd wash up when I wanted, have momma's omelettes or blintzes for breakfast, and go off to school. Now the whistle blows at 5:00 a.m., the wooden bunk shakes, straw flakes and dust clouds fly, bodies are moving every which way. We have thirty minutes to make our unmakable bed, dress in clothing that isn't clothing, wash clean with dirty water, shit when there is never any room in the shit house, get and eat breakfast of a piece of cardboard bread and a pint of piss coffee, and line up at the crazy roll call. They lined us up, must have been four thousand zebra-men, and counted us. And counted us. And counted us. Two rows over I saw two prisoners holding up a dead man to be counted. A dead man!

The worst part of today was when Mietek Szydlower, our Barrack Elder, gave us newcomers a little talk on the facts of life, I mean of death, at Maidanek. "This is a death camp," he said, "a Vernichtungslager. You've been brought here to be destroyed by hunger, beating, hard labor and sickness. You'll be eaten by lice, you'll rot in your own shit. All will end up in the big building which glows red and belches smoke." Our welcoming speech! There was no hope for almost all of us he said. The only ones who may survive more than a few months are the strongest, the ones who can "organize" a little more food here, a little less difficult work there. And be very lucky.

After his talk, our barracks was taken to the Political Department to have a record made on each of us. We walked past a big square with separate piles of all kinds of stuff - shoes, coats, pants, glasses, suitcases, books, photographs, and much more. My heart sank, was that Hilda's blue jacket in the pile near the path? Oh my God! I almost got into trouble because I didn't understand the scribe who was questioning me. He asked "What was the name of the whore that shat you into the world?" The lousy bastard! And then, after calling each of us a nobody, and treating each of us as a nobody, they made each of us nobody by taking away our names. Diary, I am no longer Lon; I am number 137376. Tatooed onto my left arm, 137376. Arrive here like a cow. Live in your own shit like a cow. And now branded like a cow.

It is all gone - momma, Hilda, home, friends, clothes, my hair, my future, my name. I turned to poppa and asked "why?" He looked at me with red, teary eyes and answered, "There is no 'why' here."

October 19

Good news and bad news. Poppa and me were given work assignments by the Arbeitsdienst this morning. Mine is very good; his is terrible. I have been made a läufer, a messenger. I am to work for the Camp Scribe, the Lagerschreiber, and take orders, files, forms, messages all over the camp. The men in my barracks say it is one of the best camp jobs for "organizing," for finding ways to get some extra food, or warmer clothing, for living a little better and maybe a little longer. We'll see. This first day was not so great. They speak so many different languages here, and the camp is big and confusing, and there are so many rules. On my first delivery I forgot and walked on a gravel path near the shoe exchange field - where prisoners try to get from each other shoes that fit - and an SS man saw me and smacked me in my face. He said the path was reserved for people, not pigs. But still, I am a läufer.

Poppa was not so lucky. After roll call, he and about 100 other new prisoners were made to do these crazy and awful exercises, strafexerzieren. Run, lie down, walk on all fours, crawl, lie on back, on belly, jump up, sit down. Over and over. Faster and faster. They call it the "race of the dead" or applying the "rule of one quarter" because the idea is to eliminate the weakest or slowest 25 men. And I mean eliminate, because the SS then kill them. They kill them for running and moving too slow!! They take them away and gas them to oblivion!! Max Straube said sometimes after the race they surround the survivors and beat them in order to eliminate still more of them, the ones that fall. Or the ones that don't move fast enough carrying the ones that fall! But they didn't do that today, and poppa by some miracle was not in the doomed 1/4. His prize for being one of the race survivors was to be put on the worst kommando, the quarry kommando. Two prisoners told us that it is the hardest, the most brutal. "Impossible stones and broken bones," they said. Poor, poor poppa. Tomorrow he will go to it; maybe it won't be so terrible.

October 23

I made a friend today, Petr. Also a läufer. I wouldn't have spoke to him, because he looks much older than me, but he spoke to me. When he asked how old I was, and I told him 15, he said "me too." I almost fainted, because he looks like an old man. It scares me very much to actually see what seven months in Maidanek can do. In a nice way he said I smell very bad, I should try to wash. Wash! There were 1000 people at the faucets this morning, and hardly any time before morning slop food and roll call. And besides, why bother when this place is so filthy, and makes us so filthy. Petr said, very seriously, that those who don't wash, who give up trying to be clean usually give up on trying to be. They die the quickest. I don't want to die. I will try to wash.

Making a friend was the only good part of the day. Poppa looks terrible. After working in the awful quarry, the SS makes all the workers bring at least one big stone back to the camp. And if it's not big enough, or you don't move fast enough, or you drop it (like poppa did) you get beaten. He's got welts on his neck, his back, and one really bad one over his eye. I wish I had a machine gun or a bag of grenades!

I got a can of sardines today from the place they call Canada, a big square and warehouse where they sort out all the clothes and stuff they take from people from the trains before they lead them down the Himmelstrasse, "the road to heaven." A prisoner gave it to me and asked me to take a message for him to his brother in camp two my next time through there. Poppa and Petr and I ate every speck in the can, and saved the can for who knows what.

Tonight, SS Untersturmführer Kaulanus made us each write postcards, like a child away at a camp or on holiday. Postcards! We are in hell, with death our daily room-mate, and we must tell loved ones all over Europe about this "fine labor camp," and "how well the Reich treats us," and the "fresh air" and "good health." I wrote my lies to Aunt Feliksa in Bialystok, and my Lvov cousins. It is only here, in this diary, where this pen can write the truth of the Gamels - living skeletons we are all to become, starvation rations and the sounds of smacking lips at night as we dream of fine foods; the cruelty of the SS, the Kapos, and so many others; and the "inscriptions from the grave" carved over my bunk and down the wall. A tombstone with a Star of David, a column of names and dates and places. A farewell to a mother. Love to a sweetheart. Initials. A begging of forgiveness. And cry after cry for revenge and witness. Last words, last wishes, last remembrances from those here before me, now gone up in smoke! I have heard that sometimes the

Germans call us meeresschaum, sea foam, because like the spray from the waves they plan that we will all disappear in the wind. Are they right, will only our carved initials and goodbyes be left?

Petr had no one to write to. His entire family, close and distant, had been taken in convoys. He came to Maidanek with his brother Elie. Their train arrived late in the evening, and when that happens, when a convoy arrives after dark and the selection can't be made and names recorded, the new prisoners are made to lie all night in the field between camps three and four. All night, face in the dirt, if you lift your head you get the top blown off by a bullet. At first light, Elie awoke from a fitful sleep and lifted his head to greet the dawn. A shot from the guard tower rang out and Elie was no more. Petr had no one to write to.

<u>October 27</u>

Poppa is being worked to death. The quarry is a killer. Every day fewer men come back alive than go out in the morning. They carry heavy, heavy loads up from the pit, and get whipped and beaten if someone thinks they're slow. Poppa's back has fresh welts every day, and the old ones don't seem to be healing. He is so weak. After work and a long, long roll call last night, our barrack was given "fatigue labor," carrying manure and then doing double time running in place. I don't even know why we were being punished. We are all beyond exhaustion.

Sleep does not refresh us. Nights are chilly now, and we are forbidden to wear anything but our shirts at night. They even had an inspection last night of what we all were wearing. One of the men in the bunk below me was wearing his pants and socks but it didn't matter, when they pulled him out of the bed to whip him, he was dead. Warmer from the clothes on, but dead! We had to drag him to roll call this morning to be counted.

I do get a little extra food for poppa, yesterday it was a bread ration, but he is going downhill, and I can't stop it. He talks to me more and more about momma. And about seeing her. Last night he showed me a cyanide pill he smuggled into the camp! It has had quite a journey he said - from home to here in the shoulder pad of his jacket, through the first day of inspection wrapped in paper in his mouth, and since then resting in the straw of his mattress. He handled it like it was a diamond.

If my words are correct - terrible, terribler, terriblest - every few days there is a new terriblest. Yesterday I was taking a package to the SS laundry hut and I passed by Canada again. One prisoner was opening suitcases from Tuesday's convoy and as I watched him, he fell over in a faint. As he fell he knocked over the suitcase he had just opened and a dead child rolled out. Is God, as poppa says, the great absentee here? A child, smuggled in by some loving parent....dead in a valise!

<u>November 1</u>

Poppa died yesterday. Rest in peace dear poppa, we will meet again soon.

<u>November 4</u>

Momma, Hilda, poppa. The last few days I have been in an envelope, not feeling my feelings. Petr's arm has been on my shoulder, but I am ALONE. Maybe poppa is the lucky one. A bullet in the neck for falling behind. Giles Spiegel from his kommando said they were forced to do "singing horses" on the trip back to camp, all the men hitched to the stone wagon, pulling it the two miles while singing the idiot German song about the joy of work. Poppa couldn't do it, or do it fast enough, or strong enough, or loud enough, and they made him and the bullet part of the load.

I am ALONE.

November 5

Blockspeere! At dawn they sealed our block, locked all doors, covered all windows. It was a death selection. No one was allowed in or out of the barrack. We were all made to get naked except for shoes and wait for the doctor. It was cold, and the wait was long. Many prisoners, especially those in the camp a long time, did things to look healthier or stronger for the selection, since mostly the weak or ill or frail are taken to the gas. They pinched or rubbed their thin cheeks, or tried to get color in them by jumping up and down or running in place. Some shaved. One man used some rouge he must have gotten from a Canada valise. Someone said the selection was no surprise to him, they always happen on Jewish holidays.

The talk scared me very much, though everyone seemed to be reassuring themselves that they wouldn't be taken. Young people said old would be taken, low numbers said high numbers would go, well people said the sick.

Then the doctor and his clerk came in. We had to line up near the Tagesraum, the Quartermaster's office, and file past them rapidly, with our arms in the air. (Afterwards, another prisoner said that the doctor was "selecting by the washboard." If the ribs stick out and can be seen clearly, your number goes on the gassing list.) The whole thing, maybe 400 men, took only 15 minutes! File past, looking as strong and healthy as you can. If the doctor told the clerk to write down your number, the clerk stopped you, copied the number from your arm, and took a quick look in your mouth.

I tried to walk past with a bouncy step, with my chest out and muscles tight. I was not written down, nor was Petr. I hugged him and he hugged me back. But the men selected stood apart, abandoned by the world. Some wept. Some prayed. I asked someone why the clerk stamped a number on the chests of some of the men selected. He said that happened to those with gold teeth, that after the gas but before the oven, the Sonderkommando "dentists" would know whose mouth to pry open in order to yank out more gold for Berlin.

November 6

I heard Hitler on the radio at home, twice - before they forbid all Jews to have radios. It really used to upset everyone, especially grandpa, to hear him rant and rave, but still, they turn the dial. One of the times it was Hitler's birthday, and he went on and on, LOUD, about how the Jews did this, and did that, and were vermin, and all kinds of terrible things. He promised to teach the Jews a lesson, he promised to punish all Jews in hundreds of different ways, he promised to make Germany Judenrein, Jew clean. On the packed train to Maidanek poppa said that unlike all the other Germans who lied to us about everything, Hitler was working hard to keep his promise.

Yesterday, I saw that poppa was right.

<u>November 8</u>

The days roll by. It is hard to know exactly how long I've been here. I think about a month. Tomorrow will be like today. Barely enough to eat. Organize to survive. Death. It is a death variety show. Some days, shoot. Other days, gas. Sometimes, the electric fence. Other times, beat to death. Most times, just waste away. One change - people seem more irritable, restless, suspicious, even more selfish. They call it the "barbed-wire sickness."

There have been more suicides in the barracks. At night, late at night, you hear the word "now", and a friend kicks the box out from under someone who put a belt over a beam and around his neck. It is hard to believe, but Stefan Bedocha did such a favor for his own father! When I got up to piss last night I had to walk with my arms in front of my face so I wouldn't bang into a hanging body in the dark.

I must try to keep thinking of the future, that there will be a future. Will I be alive after the war? Will I have an adulthood, an old age? What will the world be like 50 years from now, in 1992? Will the meadow my friends and I always loved to play in still be there? Will I have enough potatoes to eat? Will I live in America? Will Hitler, or his son be King of the world? Will all the Jews be gone? Will everyone be blond and speak German? Will anyone know I lived?

<u>November 9</u>

I remember going to a restaurant once with momma and poppa. We had to wait for a table and I kept watching the people at the one we were to sit at finish their desert and leave. They were strange looking in an interesting way, and I began to think how interesting it would be if the table could talk - about the hundreds or thousands of people who had sat around it. The conversations - deals, arguments, happy talk, sad talk, small talk, big talk. The meals eaten in silence. The secrets revealed. The dumb jokes told. Sex talked about. Sex begun. Life decisions made, at that very table.

Tonight my fantasies are similar...about my bunk. Who has lain here before, and who will lay here when I have gone up the chimney? Old men? Boys like me? And how many...ten, fifty, more? Did they, now all gone, hope to live, hope to live till the end? Did they hate, did they cry, or did they freeze their feelings and feel nothing? Did a banker sleep here, a teacher, a farmer? Were any of my bunk ancestors tailors like poppa? Were there any boys my age? Which of the names carved into this wall were boys? Did they also come here with their fathers, and watch their fathers die? Did I know any of them, from my school, from home? Senta and Erich were taken weeks before we were, did they wind up here - in this camp, this bunk?

How many will come after me? Will I be the last or will a hundred follow? Will their dreams also remain just dreams, and never become real? Will any of them know that I slept here, that I too am one of <u>their</u> bunk ancestors. Diary, good night. I am going to cut my initials, deep, into the wall beam with the others.

<u>November 10</u>

I saw a bird today, a free and flying bird. It came from the North, from the direction of the death ovens' smoke. Do I imagine too much here, or did it come from the ovens itself? It circled, it swooped, it drifted on the wind, it circled more, it played, it climbed, it dove, it seemed to be seeking a place to land. It flew toward the electrified fence, and I whispered, "Not there proud bird, please not there." It circled the treeless field, flew back toward the fence, and gently landed on it. I waited, my eyes nearly shut in apprehension, for the crisping, crackling sound of burning death I had heard twice before at human hands. But there were none. No death noises. I looked, now wide-eyed. The bird sat contentedly on the barbed wire, looked back at me, and chirped a brief sweet song. In a moment it took off again, unharmed,, toward the smoke of the dead. "Bird," I now said out loud, "you are a läufer yourself, and I thank you deeply for the message you so bravely delivered - of life from death, and of taking courage, maybe even hope - from the smoke. I will try not to forget you läufer bird. My sad heart has a little smile on it today.

November 11

The SS is furious, and some of us may pay with our lives, but we have something we have never had in Maidanek, a hero! In fact, if the stories are true, Zuckerberg is a double hero, first escaping a selection, and then from the camp itself. On the first day of Rosh Hashana, before I came to the camp, there was a selection. It was a big selection The Doctor playing God pointed to Zuckerburg as one of the men to go to the gas. But Zuckerberg noticed that the clerk following the doctor and writing down the numbers of the doomed didn't copy the numbers from the prisoners' arms, as was usually done. Instead, maybe because the doctor was going so fast, he asked prisoners to tell him their numbers. Zuckerberg made up a number! He made one up! At roll call later in the day, when the prisoners for the gas were being gathered, this number was called. No one answered. It wasn't even a Maidanek number! They probably punished the SS clerk for mis-recording!!

But Zuckerberg, ex-prisoner Zuckerberg, was more than clever. He was also very, very brave. Escape from Maidanek is very difficult. Most who have tried - under the trains, or in the piles of clothes and stuff being sent back to Germany, or in other ways - have failed. Zuckerberg invented a new way. In Camp Two is the Maidanek "hospital." Though it is called "hospital," and even has a big red cross on it, it really is used as just one more piece of the German killing machine. Many of the prisoner-patients who wind up there are killed there, usually by gasoline or phenol injection, and their bodies are thrown in the big ditch right next to the hospital. Zuckerberg noticed a number of things about the ditch. First, that the bodies thrown in were burned at irregular intervals, not every day, but when enough bodies had accumulated. Second, since the hospital was not very far from Canada, the ditch was also used to burn documents and photographs taken from each new convoy. Third, spreading the sulphur to ignite the bodies and paper, and burning them, was so unpleasant that the Ukrainian guards were usually drunk, especially by the end of each day. Finally, the wire fence next to the ditch was not electrified.

Zuckerberg managed to get into the Canada kommando and, one day, took a pile of photos and papers to the ditch and, when the guards weren't looking (he may have had help from another prisoner in distracting the guards, but stories on this differ), he threw the papers and himself into the ditch. The dangers were great - being seen by the guards, passing out from the stench as he crawled under the bodies to wait till dark, and being burned to death if he had chosen a day when the sulphur was to be spread and all the bodies incinerated. Zuckerberg was not only brave, but also very lucky, because that day was not a burning day, and as far as anyone can tell he actually escaped.

We all hope his luck continued, because a weak and skinny man, in dirty zebra clothing, with his head shaved and maybe a few gold coins in his pocket has escaped into an unfamiliar world of frightened, indifferent, or hostile farmers and townspeople. Good fortune brother Zuckerberg, and to those brave enough to follow. Tell the world we are in here!

<u>November 12</u>

Diary, tonight I tell you all about piss and shit here in the Maidanek hotel. Since mostly what they feed us is cabbage soup, water and coffee - which we call acorn cocoa - and at any one time probably half of us have dysentery and diarrhea, we do an awful lot of pissing and shitting. At night, because so many are so weak and it is so crowded, many piss or shit in their food bowls. If SS catches you, your menu of "rewards" is 25 lashes, or kneeling on the gravel outside all night, or standing all night holding bricks over your head. <u>They</u> pick. If you get up and go to the piss bucket by the front door, and the night guard thinks it's full, you get "elected" to carry it to the latrine. Some of us have gotten good at decoding the piss music from our bunks. We listen to others pissing and can tell how full the bucket is. If it's near the top, we wait for some pissing zugangi to come along and get stuck with emptying it. Between the pissing and shitting in the bowls at the bunks, and the slopping over of the pails, by most mornings the smells are piercing even for our dulled noses, and our walking around has dragged crap all over the barracks floor. This is our usual good morning greeting! It seems that the only time we don't smell it is when we have the worse smell of our brothers and sisters burning in the ovens.

Daytime pissing and shitting is much more dangerous. First we need permission from an SS to go to the latrine, and anytime you ask an SS <u>anything</u>, anything can happen. Then you have to get past the Scheissmeister, the Shitmaster. He's a poor bastard old man prisoner who they've dressed up in a rabbi frock and an odd top hat and a clock around his neck. Before we can sit on the boards of the stink hole which is our toilet, we have to salute him. We get three minutes by his clock to do our business. If we're not out and an SS is around to check, we both get beaten. The old man is shamed at every night roll call, when they make him give the shit report.

It is very, very crowded in the latrine, and sometimes people can't help shitting or pissing on another prisoner. The wait is sometimes so long that many shit in their pants, their <u>only</u> pants. There is no toilet paper, tho' some of us try to use a rag we wash out when we can. Three different times since I've been here, SS came by when I was in the latrine. Everyone runs. Twice they just yelled and whipped, once they threw two men into the cesspool and wouldn't let anyone help them out. Mietek said that they've drowned at least ten men just that way since he came here eight months ago.

At night, the Scheisskommando has to empty the shit pits and carry it all away and dump it. They are given only small pails to work with. It is a slippery pit and if they fall in, just like when someone gets thrown in in daytime, no one is allowed to pull them out. When the pit is emptied, the remaining shit kommando workers get to pull out the new corpses.

That's the whole shitty story!

November 14

Happy bithday to me,
Happy birthday to me,
Happy birthday dear 137376
Happy birthday to me

November 15

Sometimes they kill us with the deep wounds of bullets or the gas or poison injections, but sometimes ours is the death of the thousand little cuts. There were three causes for the whippings at roll call this morning. One prisoner had broken the great territory law of no one being allowed in the barracks during daytime. He went back to get, or at least look for, his spoon, and a kapo caught him. A second great and terrible criminal looked up from his "gardening" work at the commandant's house when the commandant's wife went out the door. For the crime of staring at her, 25 lashes. And, I guess because there has been a shortage lately of such awful crimes committed, we were introduced today to what I hereby name "no reason whipping." The SS came down the line and pulled out every tenth prisoner for 15 lashes. One prisoner volunteered to take the lashes for his brother, so they whipped both of them. Maidanek is a nightmare with no end.

November 17

I had this wonderful-awful dream again last night. I was in Gutmann's Bakery back home. Mr. Gutmann was making all kinds of cookies, by the hundreds. By the thousands. There were cookies everywhere - chocolate, vanilla, with cherries, with sprinkles, big cookies, little cookies, with powdered sugar, with shiny glaze. Gutmann kept giving them to me - to pack, to stack, to put in the case, and to eat. I held them, I served them, I did all kinds of things with them - but everytime I tried to eat one I couldn't find my mouth. I tried and tried and tried. I shoved one and another and still others where my mouth should be, but couldn't get any in. In the dream it made me very, very unhappy.

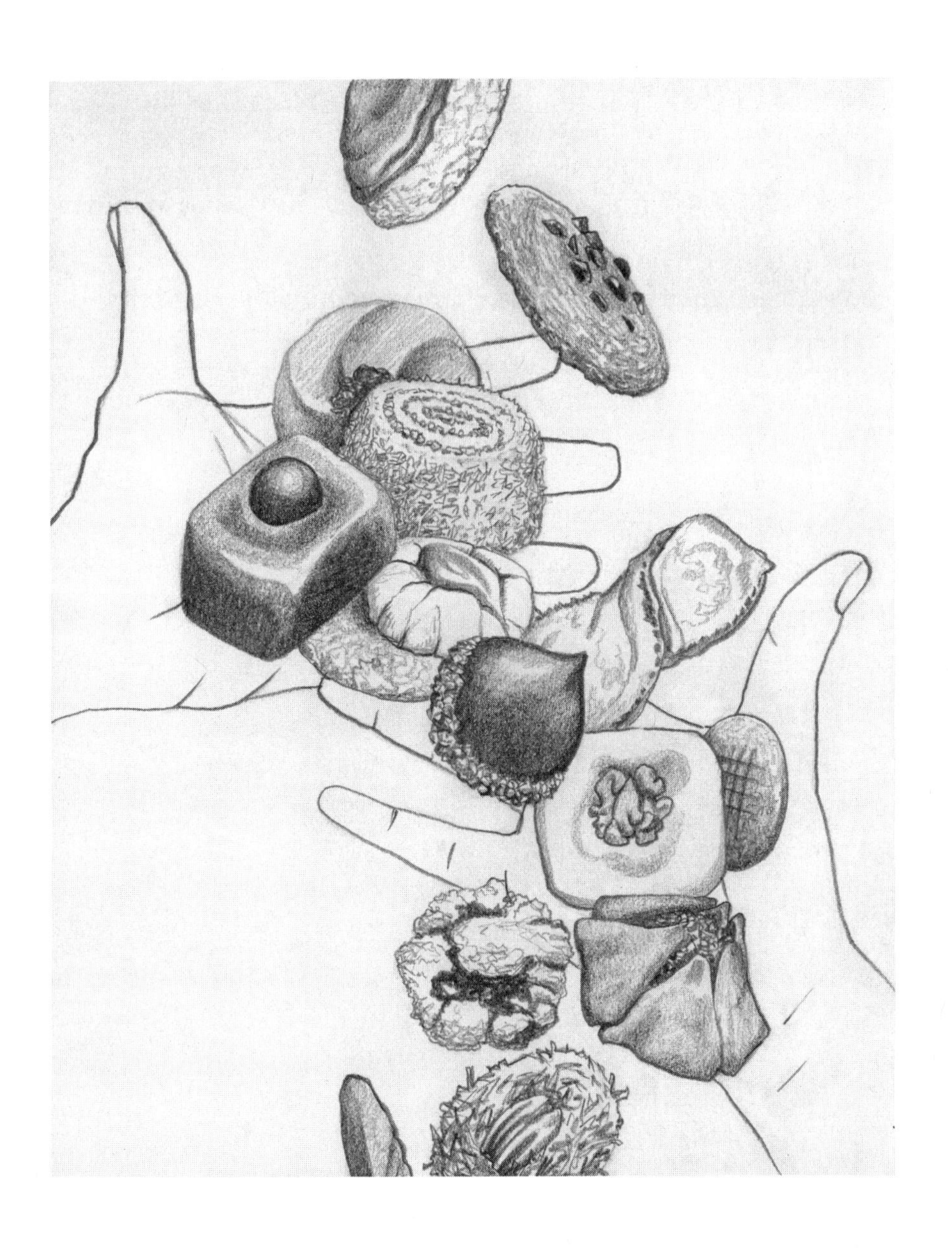

November 18

Next to me at the Appelplatz this morning was a skin and bones Muselman with a fire breathing dragon tattooed on his chest. The tattoo must have been thirty years old, and his skin was so saggy and thin and yellow that not only he, but the dragon too looked like it had collapsed into a faded, jumbly heap.

Today, like every day, after roll call it is parade time. All the kommandos, even the one poppa used to be part of, parade off to their day of slavery. Our uniforms are quite different from those the SS wear, or from the Hitler youth back home when they paraded, but in our mismatched shoes and ragged clothes we march off. The camp orchestra plays, but in our hearts we are usually people without music. Today was different though, and our march off was proud and even a bit brisker, because of the rumor that Hitler was dead. But like all the rumors here of better food or warmer clothes, Hitler the cat has nine lives.

November 19

They do so much here to make us feel so little. Clean the streets with our hands while shovels and brooms lie unused at the streetside. Clear the weeds near the commandant's house on our hands and knees with our teeth, though there are tools of all kinds in his shed. Stand naked hour after hour at roll call. Salute, bow, scrape, obey. Accept cruel punishment without complaint. Punish each other. Sing gay songs when we feel miserable. Eat, sleep, and shit like wild animals. It is no wonder we seek whatever meager ways we can to be people, not dogs. To have an actual say in something, anything, about our own lives. A man in our barracks who has been bald for years and years brags that they can never shave his head! Two others, both suicides last week, were heard to say that they, not the Germans, will decide when they will die. The man who tried to put a towel in his pants protecting his ass the morning he knew he'd get 25 lashes. And all the escape planning, revenge planning, after-the-war-return-to-the-world planning. I guess people really need to own themselves, or at least a little piece of themselves.

<u>November 20</u>

It is Sunday. In fact it is an every-other-Sunday, so we have half a day free from work. Our vacation! The SS organized a soccer game today!! It is hard to believe, but the SS produced a ball, took the läufers and the Waldkommando to the big field near the train landing and told us we could play soccer. Soccer in a death camp!

I love soccer. Most of us läufers were younger than most of them, and their work in the forest has worn several of them down. But it was still a spirited game. We won 3-1, and I scored one of the goals!! It was great fun.

Yet it was weird. A little into the game a convoy arrived, and we went on playing. Right across the fence, during the first quarter, maybe 500 souls, 500 new cattle got tossed off the train, de-baggaged, sorted liveleft and deathright, and marched away. In two hours this afternoon, the Waldkommando lost their game; 400 people lost their lives. The camp orchestra was forced to play near the crematorium to drown out their screams. And we went on playing soccer.

<u>November 22</u>

I wish I could bark and wag my tail. Delivering to the carpenter shop today I saw an SS officer feeding his dog meat - real meat, milk and an egg. I haven't seen an egg in months and the German bitch dog gets to eat one! Organizing has been hard lately since no convoys have come in in over a week. I think I could eat the damn dog! There was a dead mouse under the bunk next to me yesterday, but I couldn't do it. A group of the men near me in the barrack share recipes and imagine great meals and they did it last night. They call it "dining out," and they went on and on about gefulte fish, roast geese, salami, breads and rolls, rich desserts. It really made me hunger more, but they seem to get full somehow with their imaginations so I didn't say anything. Right now I'd even be happy for a "ghetto salad" dish of wilted beet leaves and rotten potatoes!

Today was a special torture day. Another man tried to escape and they kept us all at roll call, <u>naked</u>, until he was caught. They made another prisoner whip him, and then they painted iodine on his wounds. God, did he cry out. They made him, the man being whipped, count off each stroke and say "thank you" after the last. Then they dragged him to the gallows in the center of the roll call square and hung him. They hoisted him onto a stool, put the noose around his neck, tightened it and kicked out the stool. He yelled out "My body dies, my spirit lives. Bear witness!" The trap opened and he twisted and wiggled horribly. The kapos made all, what, 4000 of us file past him, and they made sure we turned our heads and looked at him full in the face. He was still sort of quivering when I walked past and his eyes were so bulgy. It was terrible. The man behind me said, "Where is God now?"

We got our own torture. After soup, I mean "soup", Kaulanus came in and yelled "mail call." I couldn't believe it, because it was the first time I saw that happen. But he had a stack of letters and began reading the names on the envelopes. But instead of giving them out, he put them in a pile on the dirt floor and after reading the last name he burned them. He struck a match and burned them, including the letter I got from I don't know who. Someone wrote me and I don't know who. At the end, the son of a bitch took one more letter out of his pocket, held up the open envelope and called out to one prisoner, "Your brother died." The prisoner called out "Which one?" He answered, "Take your pick." and threw that letter too into the fire.

<u>November 23</u>

I shouldn't have been so surprised, because it seems all Jews will wind up here or places like it, but I actually saw Mr. Szykier, my high school art teacher! Right here in Maidanek. In the six months since I last saw him he became ten years older. I asked him about news from home, but he answered me with a kind of far away look and a little speech about his being part of the cosmos, ageless, timeless, merging with everyone and everything - past, present and future. He talked about each of us being but a cup of water in a flowing stream. I'm not sure I understood his meaning, but it sounded like something I should think about hard.

November 24

Do we have lice, or do the lice have us? They bite us when they want, where they want, how often they want. They live wherever they wish in our clothes, our hair, our skins, our stinking sores. We tell them to go away, to visit with the Germans for a while. But either lice don't hear too well or they know the Germans taste too sour. So they stay, they keep on bleeding us, and with each bite they make it clear that in Maidanek the lice have people, not the other way around.

November 25

All at once the barrack is very crowded. There were about 400 in here and I bet they've almost doubled it. It is very crowded. Three convoys came in the last two days, and for whatever reason they're sending less to the gas. Maybe they need more workers for something, or maybe the truck with the red cross that brings the gas just broke down. Whatever, I now sleep with two other people in my bunk. Petr and I were crowded before. Now we must sleep on our side and, if one moves, all three must move. I used to think it couldn't be more crowded than it was the last few months at home before they came for us. They had a rule, "six Jews to a window." For every window a room had, six people were assigned to the room. Our bunk here feels like a three window room! And right after that most terrible time of every day, when we wake up and realize all over again where we are and what we face, there is a mad arms and legs scramble all over the barrack to get going. A madhouse. It is the best example of one of the worst things about being here, never, never being alone.

Today a kapo found some gold coins buried in a barrack. There was an immediate roll call and with great anger, Havick from the Death's Head guards warned us under threat of our lives not to have any gold, silver, rings, watches or documents. An SS man saw a few coins near the feet of one prisoner. I don't know if they were his, but they grabbed him and pushed him into the electrified fence. He just hung there, standing up, fried and died. Then they made all of us march in front of Havick, who every now and then would pull someone out to be searched. I found out later that a man in our barrack had a false Aryan birth certificate which he tore into little pieces in his pocket and, while the line was moving, he ate it.

<u>November 26</u>

Food is getting harder and harder to find. Everyone is so hungry. The watery soup is more and more almost all water. Scraps, garbage and the leftovers(!) from the very sick have all but disappeared. It was very dangerous, but some were using gold or jewelry found in the Canada to buy food from the Christians who live near the camp. At night they'd go to the latrine, real late, and stick their hands through the hole in the fencewall. An unseen arm would take the gold and put some food in their hand - a sausage, or bread, a potato, or something. I got this potato that way two days ago. It is my treasure and I am saving it. Last night the SS found out about the hole, some fucking informer maybe, and was waiting - butcher knife at the ready for the hands to come through the hole. At least four prisoners were sliced before closing down word got around, at least in our barrack. This morning at roll call the SS made everyone show their arms and the four men with cuts were dragged away to whatever new hell the SS have arranged.

I am so hungry. I can't think about anything but the potato. It has a bump on it. I must save the potato, but maybe I'll just eat the bump. If I do, can I stop at just the bump? Maybe I should just lick it to get the flavor. Or smell it, to get its aroma. I think I'll shove the whole wonderful potato in my mouth and wolf it down, like I had 20 of them. No, nibbling, slow-nibbling, would be best. It's small, but I can make it last two or three hours. A better idea, eat half of it today, half tomorrow. I love to hold it, suck on it. It is my potato, my treasure.

Last year, poppa took a potato, made a hole in it, poured oil in the hole, stuck in a braided wick and used it as a Chanukah candle. For sure, if I had that candle now I would eat it.

<u>November 27</u>

Does hell have a hell? Is there a bottom under the bottom? It is the nightmare of all nightmares. My brain has learned to let in all kinds of worsts, but just will not register what has happened. I think of its horror and a mind curtain descends.

All last week large groups of prisoners were taken off their kommandos and in groups of maybe 300 made to dig three huge ditches. They are right near the fence of camp three, each maybe two yards deep and 1000 yards long. This morning they started wiping out most of the camp, and I cannot understand why I am still alive. Poppa was right, there is no "why." About 100 SS, armed to the teeth, took group after group of almost 100 prisoners each to one of the ditches. I watched through my tears. They made them undress, and pushed them into the ditch alive - then they raked the ditch with German bullets from German machine guns. Then another hundred was pushed in on top of the last 100, and another barrage of bullets. And another and another.

At first the screams were horrible. My soul cried, and cried out. Then the butchers brought in a sound truck, and played loud marches, ballads, even dance tunes to cover up the screaming. Music to die by.

Thousands of my people, of all our people, died in agony today. We must have our day of revenge, and it must be a day of a thousand knives, a million cuts, a day of ultimate pain for <u>them</u>. Sorrow fills my heart, fear stirs my pulse, hate envelopes me.

<u>November 28</u>

Can someone die more than one time? I think the answer is <u>yes</u>. We have. We died when they first stormed our house and took or broke our lifetime of everything. We died again when they forced us out, into the filthy ghetto. We died again there, and slowly, as little food became no food. We died a fourth death at the roundup, when grandpa died, a fifth on the train, a sixth when it stopped, a seventh when momma and Hilda were taken away, an eighth when poppa, died, and on, and on, and on. Sure someone can die many, many times.

And so too must they die again and again. Death without end. We must first line them up at a trench they have dug, look them in the eyes and shoot them right in the face. Then when they are thoroughly dead, we shall alive them and hang them till they are dead for a second time. We will bring them back again, and put them in a locked barracks with no food or water till they starve to death. Alive them again, and off to work at the ovens, burning their own parents and children. Then burn them alive till they are dead again. And on and on forever. Never a final death; always one more painful death waiting.

November 30

I used to love the dawn. It was a kind of fresh quietness, a newness, a hopefulness, sometimes even a sense of both. Plans for the day soon to arrive, or even on days without plans. Now dawn is grim, not smiling; black, not beckoning. Dawn in Maidanek is a dawn of death, not life, despair, not hope. They rob me of so much here, of my everything here, even the dawn.

<u>December 1</u>

Today seems to be a death vacation day! So many died last week. I hear no shots. The oven's not glowing; the stacks aren't blowing. I haven't seen a dead body all day. (Did I really once write in this diary that I was a death virgin!!) Petr, Emil, Tadus and I had only a few deliveries, and the sun was shining all day - which doesn't happen so often in Poland in December. The winter under-jacket I got yesterday from some Greek fellow for a bowl and spoon is keeping me really warmer. My weight is really down a lot, and I'm feeling colder these days, so I need it.

The one meal yesterday was "German pineapples" (turnips for good teeth only!) and what looked like very old cabbage leaves and what Emil said were pine tree shoots. Today it was the usual "soup", but we worked the soup strategy just right. If it's potato or turnip soup - which settles to the bottom (the kapo <u>never</u> stirs deep), get toward the end of the line in order to get more "thick". If it's cabbage, nettles or other so-called vegetables that float, get toward the front. We eat it right away, because any food put down in Maidanek, even for a moment, is gone, crammed into one or another yellow skin face with sunken eyes and cheekbones sticking out.

Today the four of us delivered a beautiful bed, made in the carpenter shop from special woods, to the Obersturmfuhrer's cottage right outside the main gate. When we picked it up at the shop, it looked like they were working on a big matching cabinet too. Tadus started telling about the time he visited his great aunt in Kolo and slept in a bed almost as nice. It was a lovely story, but made us all very sad.

December 2

If the Germans can do magic with their guns and planes like they do with their bread, they will win the war for sure. First of all, Erling at the camp bakery told me it is made mostly of sawdust, along with some turnip flour. Not wheat, not oats, not rye, but from worthless sawdust and spoiled turnips. Second, it is the only bread ever baked that is never fresh. Even as it comes from the oven it is stale. Instant hard and stale.

Then it comes time to divide it, and more magic. It is, if I have the words right, infinitely divisible. No matter how thin the slice, even if you can see clearly through it, it can be sliced again. We have had half rations of half rations of half rations. Next, yet one more magical miracle. The more you eat, the hungrier you get. If you let your empty stomach sleep, you are only very, very hungry. But if you wake it up with a see-through slice of stale German sawdust bread, the hunger becomes almost too much to bear.

Finally, the greatest bread magic of all. Hocus pocus, the bread gets bigger and smaller, smaller and bigger, all by itself depending on in whose hand it is held. This has happened to other prisoners, and it has happened to me. A piece of bread gets carefully divided in half. You look at your piece and the other person's and you are convinced that his "half" is bigger. But magic, he thinks the same thing about your piece! So you agree to trade, and after you give him your "smaller" piece for his "bigger" piece, and look at the piece that was yours now in his hands, you swear that once again he has the bigger piece! Incredible German stale, sawdust, eat more get hungrier, shrinking swelling bread. MAGIC.

<u>December 3</u>

Sometimes luck smiles; sometimes it kills. Geert Prudkij, an "old" läufer (only God can judge actual ages here!) was selected for the gas. His legs were swollen with water and when Dr. Hippke pressed his finger on it it made a dent. For a dent you die here, so his number was written down. He was taken with the others to an empty barrack, and packed in like feeble sardines for two days with no food or water. Yesterday they were taken down the Himmelstrasse, and locked into the gas chamber. They stayed there, praying, weeping, confessing, imploring, or quietly, for two hours waiting for the end. Tonight I played a game of checkers with him at the back of our own barracks! Run out of killing gas? Crematoria ovens broken? Too many corpses laying around? Who knows, Hitler didn't call Geert on the phone to explain. After the two hours they unlocked the doors, and dragged the entire selection back to their barracks. Hello life, surprised to see you again.

Luck also kills, and I saw it with my own eyes. A prisoner I never saw before, or at least didn't recognize, just walked around a corner and almost knocked into an SS Rottführer who seemed quite drunk, even though it was still morning. The SS kicked at the man, then grabbed his striped cap and sailed it toward the electric fence. It landed only a foot or two from the fence. "Get the hat pigshit or I will send your head after it with the help of a bullet!" The prisoner became a statue. "I will be shot from the guard tower if I get within two yards of that fence," he screamed back in fear. "I will protect you. I give you permission." said the SS. The man didn't move, but the SS, turning red with anger and liquor shoved the man, toward the fence. The man, stumbling from the shoves, moved closer and closer to that two yards of no-man's land. He fell to the ground about five yards out, and dug into the dirt, holding on to it. The SS shot twice in the air, the man - turning white as a ghost - got up and ran toward the fence. Just as he lurched forward, almost grasping the hat, a shot rang out from the tower and the man fell in a spurting pool of his own blood. Hello death, surprised to meet you too.

December 4

The Steblinskis and Sadiks went to America two Decembers ago. I wonder how Albin and Wasil are, and Hilda's best friend Eva. The letter momma got from Wasil and Eva's mother said it was a hard life, hard to fit in. I wonder how they are. I wonder what they ate for supper tonight. Would they, so far away on another planet, believe all this? Would they believe any of this? I wonder if they ever think of me, of Hilda, of momma and poppa.

December 5

People here don't like to talk much about who and what they were before they came here. Some, the ones most starved out, don't even remember. For others, those whose families went up the chimney, remembering hurts too much. Still others, when they lost their names for numbers, they lost their histories too. But it comes out one way or another for many of them. In my barrack, there are at least three or four tailors like poppa. Two doctors, three professors, a bricklayer, several farmers, two grocers, two teachers, an animal doctor, an actor, a man's barber and a lady's barber, and at least a half dozen bosses of what I'm not sure. But in Maidanek almost everyone has changed jobs. The bosses get bossed, the barbers don't cut, the bricklayer doesn't lay, the farmers don't farm, the professors and teachers use their backs to teach the rocks how to get in the wagon at the quarry, the animal doctor doctors people at the "hospital" and the people doctors carry soup for the kesselkommando, the grocers have no groceries, the tailors have no cloth, and the only one still really in his old job is Laszlo the actor. He works at the Plage Laszkewiez, Maidanek's unloading platform for new convoys. When the terrified newcomers ask "What will happen to us?" or "What is that terrible smell?" or "Are they going to kill us?", Laszlo gives a shrug of ignorance, or a shoulder pat to reassure, and sometimes - when the SS is close - he even tells them there is nothing to worry about here in this labor camp.

December 6

I threw up my guts today! Just when you think the callouses on your heart are as thick as those on your hands, a new terror surprises. Tadus and I were on the soup line together, near the back. We were talking about how the Waldkommando is made to camouflage the sides of the road to heaven with thick branches, so that prisoners can't see in or out. It was Tadus' turn at the soup. The room senior put the ladle deep into the soup vat, just as we hoped, and came up with a human jaw!!! They have turned us into slaves, into lice factories, into skin and bones, and now into cannibals. It is too disgusting to even think about.

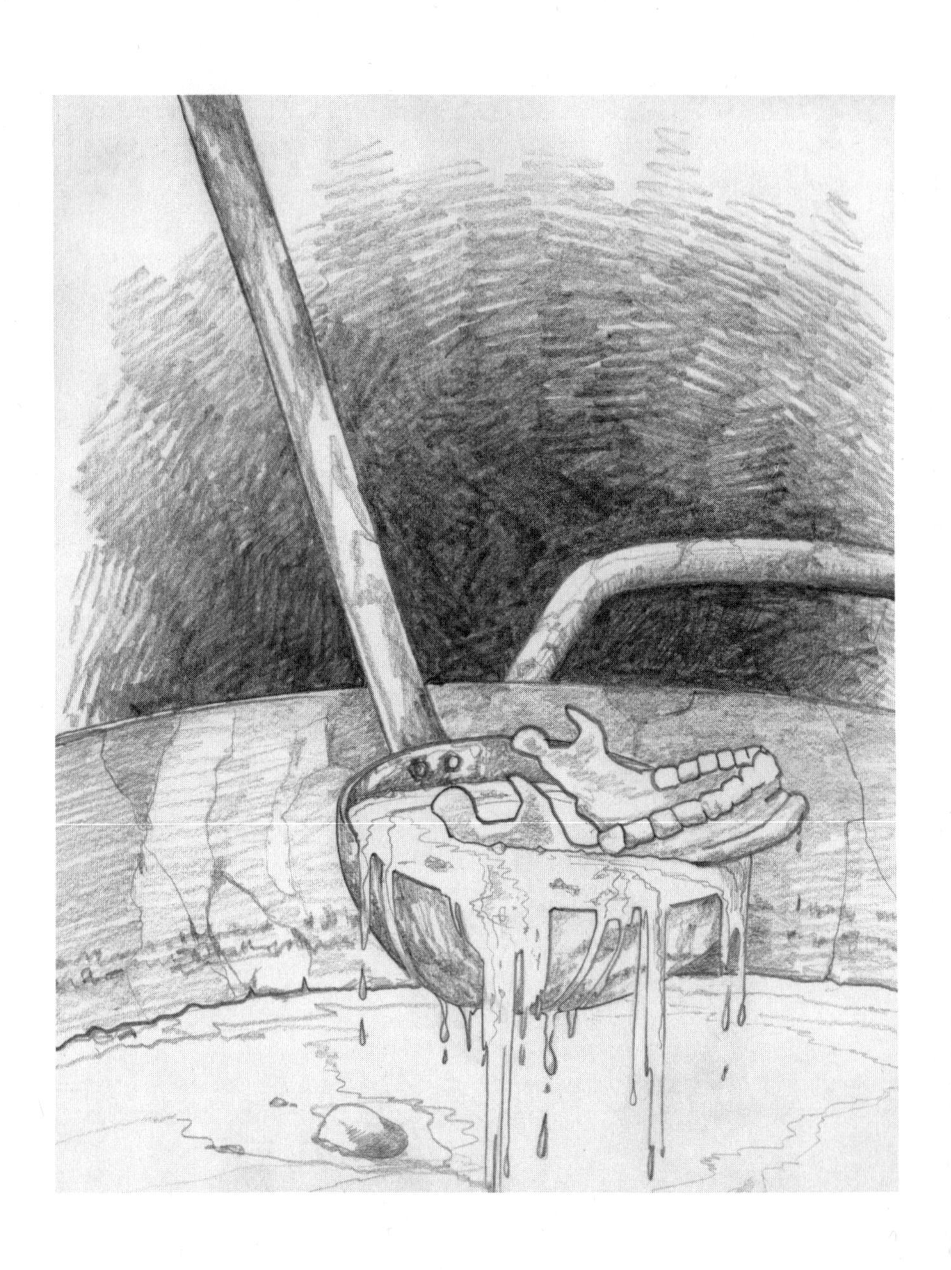

<u>December 7</u>

Who am I? Am I still a child? I must ask permission to pee or shit. I must take my hat off to every SS. I am mostly powerless, don't decide things for myself, sometimes dream of what will be. Am I still a child?

Am I now a man? I am still alive here after two months. Some days I find enough to eat. I shave when I can. I think like a man. I hate like a man. I sometimes dream of what is. Am I now a man?

Am I an old man? There is no energy left in my walk. My soccer-sprinter, two stairs at a time, run to the store for milk legs grow weaker by the day. I am tired all the time. My skin is dry and a little yellow. I am a good bit thinner. Sometimes I cry. Sometimes I dream of what was. Am I an old man now?

They shaved my head again today. About every three weeks. Someone said it was to control the lice, but I think it just makes us easier to get pointed out and brought back if we escape.

<u>December 8</u>

I hurt so much. Can't write today.

<u>December 12</u>

Four (five?) days ago I had a rare message delivery to the Sonderkommando kapo at the ovens. Alena, Tadus' sister in the women's camp has a boyfriend she was to marry who is part of the Sonderkommando and we four agreed that whoever got a message to deliver into the crematoria would try to smuggle in a note from her to him. His name is (was) Miroslav Dabek. Alena was desperate, because she found out the awful truth that each Sonderkommando is itself gassed after about three months at the ovens, and Miroslav started two weeks before I got here - in the beginning of October.

I put her note in my shoe, and went to the crematoria. I found the kapo and gave him his envelope. I waited till he was walking away and I started toward the door. I asked the first prisoner I saw to point out Dabek. He did, and I walked over to where Dabek and another prisoner were loading corpses into the end ovens. I quickly bent down to reach into my shoe, but before I could grasp Alena's note I felt a terrific blow on my back, my kidney. The kapo had seen me, and smashed me - again and again - with his studded belt. He screamed at me, called me a smuggling Jew bastard. I must have fainted, because when I came to I was in this terrible Stehzelle (standing cell).

It is cold in here, and dark, and they keep coming in to wet my shirt with ice cold water. An SS lieutenant came by and said to me "You are a lucky pig. The shit you tried to smuggle the message to has been burned alive in his own oven! Fried shit! And you would be with him, but Dr. Schumann has plans for you, ex-läufer 137376! In the meantime, we have rules in here. Follow them or 25 lashes. Do not pace. Do not look out that grille. From 5:00 AM, when the whistle blows, to 10:00 PM stand at attention facing the glass in this door. When we come by, if we don't see your pig face, 25 lashes given with pleasure."

I stood there for two days, but my legs turned to rubber and I had to half-sit against the wet and frost-covered wall. A guard saw me and rushed in and shoved me against the back wall, then pushed my face into the toilet bowl and kept it down. It was full of shit. I thought I had drowned. I could barely breathe, even afterwards. Every part of me hurts so bad. If only I had found poppa's cyanide.

December 14

I was taken today with several others to Dr. Schumann's infirmary. I needed help from Emil, who was also there, because I'm not walking too good after the cell and the beatings. They made us get naked and wait a long time on line. Most were not sick, so we couldn't even guess why we were at the infirmary. Then they started bringing us one at a time into another room. Those who went in must have either stayed where they brought them or been taken out some other door, because no one came out to explain what was going on. Mostly I didn't think it was some kind of selection, though Mietek once told me about what he called "selection by injection." Then I got taken in. A doctor and an orderly who I'd never seen before put me in front of what looked like an x-ray machine and put my penis and balls on this sort of square plate. I asked what they were doing but they told me to shut my fucking mouth. Then they held me still and I heard this buzzing noise for about five minutes. It must have been the x-ray machine. I got taken out right after that and they gave me "new" clothing. The shirt is so big I look like some dumb clown.

Diary, they brought me back to my own barracks. I was very surprised because I thought I'd be back in the cell for sure. Can you even imagine someone being happy to be back here!!

December 18

I am in great pain. I have no way to stop it. Little by little since the x-ray my penis and balls have turned black, and hurt so bad. They turned disgusting black and purple and oozing. Three days ago a young doctor butcher did surgery on me and cut off my right ball. They brought me back to the infirmary, again with several others. First they stuck a piece of wood up my ass and moved and shoved it till sperms came from my penis. I almost fainted from the pain. Then someone gave me an injection in my back. I heard a man in the next room yell "Why are you operating on me, I'm not sick!" and the same doctor who did the x-rays on me answered "Stop barking like a dog. You will die anyway." I was very, very frightened. They brought me in the room and put mc on a table and the doctor operated off my right testicle. He cut it off and then held it up to show the others.

I hurt, hurt, hurt. And I am burning up with fever. And blood is oozing from my wound. And my penis is black. Some prisoners they kill at once, some part by part. My penis, never used in love, never inside a woman, now a killed penis. I weep for me, dying part by part. I am being murdered a part at a time.

December 21

I am not to be given any peace. I am not to be allowed to recover. Petr and I are dressed in German aviator uniforms - from boots to helmets with goggles. They have put us in a tub about six feet deep and wide, filled with very cold water. Very, very cold. Something is attached to Petr's helmet which causes the back of his head to go back and be in the water. Dr. Rascher said "we now give you a very special German bath," and then stuck something up my ass, and one up Petr's. Maybe it is to see how cold we get.

I am shivering. I am shaking. It is hard to breathe, and there is so much mucous in my throat. A minute, or ten minutes ago, Petr, my dear cousin, said to me "we will not survive this one." But now he is very still. I think he is right, I grow numb. It is hard to move my arms. How long have we been in here? I am both numb and very cold at the same time, how can that be? I feel stiff. It is hard to move my arms. All Hilda could say was, "I never did anybody any harm." That bright light, a thousand Chanukah candles. How soft and warm is Tadus' Aunt's bed? I am so tired. I am so numb. I am.

At 6:42 AM on 12/22/42, the body of prisoner 137376 was dragged to the roll call square by two zugangi, to be counted along with all other living, barely living and not living prisoners.

At 8:22 AM on 12/22/42, Camp Lagerschreiber Kurtz entered the record room just down the gravel walk from the crematoria, took down Prisoner Record Book #9, turned to the first empty page, and wrote on the top line:

12/22/42 - Prisoner 137376, died while trying to escape.

At 11:02 on 12/22/42, the body of prisoner 137376 was lifted by two members of Camp Maidanek Sonderkommando eleven and thrown into the oven they were working. The burning fat of the preceding corpse rapidly caused the new fuel to catch fire.

At 11:03 AM on 12/22/42, the smoke that was prisoner 137376 went up the chimney.

Prisoner 137376, classmate to Boris, brother to Hilda, son to momma and poppa, "cousin" to Petr and, to the Germans, läufer and subject in sterilization and freezing experiments, all that remained to mark his stay in Maidanek were his initials carved with a rusty spoon into the third ceiling beam from the rear in Barrack 17 and, along with those from many thousands of other prisoners, his shoes.

Epilogue: A Letter to Lon

It is 1992, fifty years since your murder at Maidanek. The ashes that were you lie intermingled with the ashes of thousands of others, bleached by the sun of 50 Polish summers, the cold of 50 Polish winters. The smoke that was you has long joined the eternal winds of time. The fire in the ovens is out, and the SS is gone. Your barrack still stands, but its boards are gray and warped. On sunny Spring days, a ray of sunlight shines through on your very bunk. It is very quiet at Maidanek now, no screams, no gunshots, no bellowed orders. A gentle breeze stirs the soft grass, now tended by the sons of your farmer neighbors during your days here.

What remains are your shoes, and the shoes of 800,000 others. I walked among them and wept as I heard the silent footsteps they never took. They were all black, not in their birth but in their 50 years of aging. They smelled of death, not in my nostrils, but in my heart. Shoes, shoes, shoes, a cascade of shoes, a barrage of shoes, a shoe mortuary.

I came to your shoe, and gently picked it up to touch, if I could, its sole, and your soul. The penny-sized hole near the toe, did you get it from the gravel on your läufer trips, or playing in the streets of home before the camp? The lace was a third of its original length, how did you keep it on in the Maidanek mud? Lon, I spoke to your shoe, to you. I poked my pinky into the hole...to connect. I caressed your shoe and drew it to me...to tell you I know you existed, and that your life mattered, and still matters. To tell you that your shoe still leaves deep footprints, footprints that say by your death the world has had less love, less laughter, bridges unbuilt, hurts unsoothed, less joy, less humanity. Such loss is our lesson and your legacy. We hold your shoe and cry, but we will not forget. Your name is Lon, for lives on.

SOURCES

Adelson, A. & Lapides, R. (1989). Lodz ghetto. N.Y.: Viking.

Arad, Y. (1987). Blezec, Sobibor, Treblinka: The Operation Reinhard Death Camps. Bloomington, IN.: Indiana University Press.

Bernbaum, I. (1986). I am a star. New York: Simon & Schuster.

Borowski, T. (1967). This way for the gas, ladies and gentlemen. New York: Penguin Books.

Des Pres, T. (1976). The survivor. Oxford: Oxford University Press.

Donat, A. (1963). The Holocaust kingdom. New York: Holocaust Library.

Eisenberg, A. (1981). Witness to the Holocaust. New York: The Pilgrim Press.

Eliach, Y. (1982). Hasidic tales of the Holocaust. New York: Vintage Books.

Ferderber-Salz, B. (1980). And the sun kept shining... New York: Holocaust Library.

Fertig, H. (1982). From the history of KL-Auschwitz. New York: Howard Fertig Inc.

Freilich, S. (1988). The coldest winter. New York: Holocaust Library.

Geve, T. (1987). Guns and barbed wire: A child survives the holocaust. Chicago: Academy Chicago Publishers.

Gilbert. M. (1979). Final journey. New York: Mayflower Books.

Gill, A. (1988). The journey back from hell. New York: Avon Books.

Gotfryd, B. (1990). Anton the dove fencier and other tales of the Holocaust. New York: Washington Square Press.

Ka-Tzetnik 135633 (1973). House of dolls. London: Granada Pub. Ltd.

Kielar,, W. (1972). Anus mundi: 1500 days in Auschwitz/Birkenau. N.Y.: N.Y. Times Books.

Klein, C. (1988). Sentenced to live. New York: Holocaust Library.

Klein, G. W. (1957). All but my life. New York: The Noonday Press.

Kogan, E. (1950). The theory and practice of hell. New York: Berkley Books.

Korczak, J. (1978). Ghetto diary. New York: Holocaust Library.

Lanzmann, C. (1985). Shoah: An oral history of the Holocaust. New York: Pantheon Books.

Levi, P. (1959). Survival in Auschwitz. New York: Collier Books.

Nomberg-Przytyk, S. (1985). Auschwitz. Chapel Hill: University of North Carolina Press.

Rubinowicz, D. (1982). The diary of David Rubinowicz. Washington, D.C.: Creative Options.

Sandberg, M. (1968). My longest year. Jerusalem: Yad Vashem.

Topas, G. (1990). The iron furnace: A holocaust survivor's story. Lexington, Ky.: N.Y. Times Books.

Wiesel, E. (1960). Night. New York: Bantam Books.

Willenberg, S. (1989). Surviving Treblinka. Oxford: Basil Blackwell.

All royalties derived from the sale of

this book have been assigned to the

Simon Wiesenthal Center, Los Angeles, California